P9-DUV-719

Dear Parent:
Your child's love of reading starts here!

Every child learns to read in a different way and at his or her own speed. Some go back and forth between reading levels and read favorite books again and again. Others read through each level in order. You can help your young reader improve and become more confident by encouraging his or her own interests and abilities. From books your child reads with you to the first books he or she reads alone, there are I Can Read Books for every stage of reading:

SHARED READING
Basic language, word repetition, and whimsical illustrations, ideal for sharing with your emergent reader

BEGINNING READING
Short sentences, familiar words, and simple concepts for children eager to read on their own

READING WITH HELP
Engaging stories, longer sentences, and language play for developing readers

READING ALONE
Complex plots, challenging vocabulary, and high-interest topics for the independent reader

ADVANCED READING
Short paragraphs, chapters, and exciting themes for the perfect bridge to chapter books

I Can Read Books have introduced children to the joy of reading since 1957. Featuring award-winning authors and illustrators and a fabulous cast of beloved characters, I Can Read Books set the standard for beginning readers.

A lifetime of discovery begins with the magical words "I Can Read!"

Visit www.icanread.com for information
on enriching your child's reading experience.

To Annie Stone—in lieu of
a tutu, all my thanks
—J.O'C.

For Lisl—a divine dancer,
teacher, and friend
—R.P.G.

For C.I., with too-too
many layers of memory
tulle to mention
—T.E.

I Can Read Book® is an imprint of HarperCollins Publishers.

Fancy Nancy: Too Many Tutus Text copyright © 2013 by Jane O'Connor Illustrations copyright © 2013 by Robin Preiss Glasser
All rights reserved. Manufactured in China. No part of this book may be used or reproduced in any manner whatsoever without
written permission except in the case of brief quotations embodied in critical articles and reviews. For information address
HarperCollins Children's Books, a division of HarperCollins Publishers, 195 Broadway, New York, NY 10007.
www.icanread.com

Library of Congress Cataloging-in-Publication Data is available.
ISBN 978-0-06-208308-1 (trade bdg.) — ISBN 978-0-06-208307-4 (pbk.)

20 SCP 10 9 8 7 6 ❖ First Edition

O'Connor, Jane.
Fancy Nancy :too many tutus

2013
33305250588179
ca   08/08/22

I can read! ead!

BEGINNING
1
READING

Fancy NANCY

Too Many Tutus

by Jane O'Connor

cover illustration by Robin Preiss Glasser

interior illustrations by Ted Enik

HARPER

An Imprint of HarperCollinsPublishers

My closet is bulging.

That is a fancy way to say

that the door will not close.

"You have too many tutus,"

my mom tells me.

My mom wants to give some away.
"This tutu is too small for you,"
she says.

"Yes, but now I can wear this tutu

on my head.

I look like a bride!"

I say.

"This tutu is torn," my mom points out.

"But it makes a lovely cape," I say.

"See?"

Then my mom says,

"Look.

These two tutus are too small,

and they are identical."

(Identical means the same—

my mom knows fancy words too.)

"Okay, okay!" I say.

I give one tutu to JoJo.

I give one tutu to Frenchy.

My mom wants to give away more tutus.

But I refuse!

That's fancy for saying no way!

The next day Ms. Glass says,

"It is the first day of the month."

Ms. Glass is going

to measure each of us.

We all get out our growth charts.

Ooh la la!

I have grown almost an inch

since school started.

Clara is miserable.

That's fancy for very, very unhappy.

"I am not any taller," she says.

"I'm not growing!"

"Your body is growing all the time,"
Ms. Glass says.
"Only one person here
is not growing—ME!"

"One day you will stop growing, but not for a long time."

Clara looks relieved.

That's fancy for feeling better.

After our growth charts are put away,

Ms. Glass tells us about

a "swap-and-shop."

"On Thursday, bring in clothes

that you have outgrown.

You will get a point for every item."

(Item is a fancy word for thing.)

On Friday

we can spend our points on items

that other children have brought in.

Ooh la la!

I like this idea.

My mom likes this idea too!

We clean out my closet.

"What about a few tutus?"

my mom asks.

I relent.

(That is fancy for give in.)

The next morning
my shopping bag is bulging
with tutus and clothes.
Ms. Glass counts my items.
I get fifteen tickets.

The swap-and-shop is in the gym.

Will I find a long velvet dress?

Or party shoes with jewels on the bows?

Or a real cape with fake-fur trim?

I am not so sure.

Mostly I see lots of old sweatshirts and old jeans.

Then suddenly I see the tutu
of my dreams.

Oh no!

Grace sees it too.

Grace gets to the tutu first.

"Mine!" she shouts.

But Grace has only five points.

And the tutu costs seven points.

"Ha! Mine!" I say.

I start to take the tutu

from Grace.

But she looks miserable.

That makes me feel bad.

I have lots of tutus, after all.

So I give Grace two of my points.

She can buy the tutu now.

Ms. Glass takes me aside and says,

"That was very thoughtful."

(Thoughtful is fancy for kind.)

Then she says,

"You are growing up in lots of ways."

The swap-and-shop is almost over.

I still have lots of points.

I spend them all on two tutus!

What a bargain!

(That's fancy for something good
that doesn't cost a lot.)

At home

I model my new tutus.

"Two new tutus!" says Mom.

But she does not mind.

Why?

For the first time in ages,

my closet door closes!

Fancy Nancy's Fancy Words

These are the fancy words in this book:

Bargain—something good that doesn't cost a lot

Bulging—very full

Identical—the same

Item—thing

Miserable—very, very unhappy

Refuse—a fancy way of saying no

Relent—give in

Relieved—feeling better

Thoughtful—kind